Black's Munna disappears! Was it Pokémon-napped? Then Black is attacked by...a Pokémon?!

Then, can Black pull his weight in show biz as White's employee?

VOL. 4 AVAILABLE NOW!

WELL, I BETTER GET GOING...

BIANCA. Oh, she really does run a talent agency!

I'M CHEREN.

OH, HELLO! I'M WHITE. I REPRESENT THE BW AGENCY. IF YOU'RE IN SHOW BIZ, DON'T HESITATE TO CALL!

HI, BOSS. IT WENT *GREAT*. MY TWO FRIENDS HERE FOUGHT BY MY SIDE.

BYE, CHEREN! BYE, BIANCA— THANKS A LOT!

SEE YOU SOON!

AGH! WE'VE GOT TO FIND HIM— AGAIN!

HIS...WHAT? YOU DIDN'T ASK HIM, BIANCA?

NO...

CHEREN? WHAT'S BLACK'S XTRANSCIEVER NUMBER?

SIGH... SO YOU REALLY DO WORK FOR A POKÉMON TALENT AGENCY...

I'VE SEEN IT, I'VE SEEN IT! WOW!

MAYBE YOU'VE SEEN THE AD ON TV ALREADY... TEP ACTED IN A TV SERIES TOO! SOME SHOW NAMED *THE DAYS OF OUR POKÉMON*.

SOR-RY TO KEEP YOU WAITING.

TP TP TP

AT LEAST NOW WE CAN CALL HIM WHEN-EVER WE WANT, HUH, CHEREN?

HOW DID YOUR GYM BATTLE GO?

WHAT TOOK YOU GUYS SO LONG?

CHEREN KEPT THANKING THEM OVER AND OVER FOR THE GYM BATTLE AND APOLOGIZING FOR SOMETHING OR OTHER....

SURE. I UNDERSTAND.

HEY, BLACK... PROFESSOR JUNIPER WANTS TO KEEP IN CONTACT WITH YOU. SO DO WE.

THAT'S TRUE.

YOU ALWAYS DID HAVE SUPER GOOD MANNERS—EVER SINCE YOU WERE A LITTLE KID!

HERE'S ONE FOR CHEREN TOO.

HERE...

I'LL GIVE YOU AN XTRANSCEIVER.

THE COMPANY I WORK FOR HIRED OUT POKÉMON TO ACT IN A XTRANSCEIVER TV COMMERCIAL, AND THEY GAVE US LOTS OF SAMPLES.

A COMMUNICATION DEVICE.

WOW! COOL! ...WHAT IS IT?

...EVER SINCE WE STARTED WORKING ON OUR APPETIZER... OUR TEST.

WE WERE AT A DISADVANTAGE THANKS TO OUR POKÉMON TYPES AND LACK OF BATTLE EXPERIENCE, SO I'VE BEEN ON THE LOOKOUT FOR SOMETHING THAT MIGHT HELP US...

YEP.

YOU FOUND OUT ABOUT THAT TOO, DID YOU?!

I JUST WANTED TO PROVE THAT I WAS PUTTING THE ONE THAT'S STILL WORKING TO GOOD USE.

I FELT REALLY BAD ABOUT BREAKING THE OTHER TWO POKÉDEXES...

I HAD NO IDEA IT COULD BE SO HANDY IN BATTLE!

YOU WON BY USING YOUR POKÉDEX!

OH, BUT YOU'VE GOT IT ALL WRONG...

WELL DONE, BLACK!

...THE TRIO BADGE!

THE SYMBOL OF YOUR VICTORY AND PROOF OF YOUR POKÉMON TRAINER SKILLS...

WHATEVER THE MOTIVE, YOU WON THE BATTLE. YOU'VE DONE WELL. HERE YOU GO!

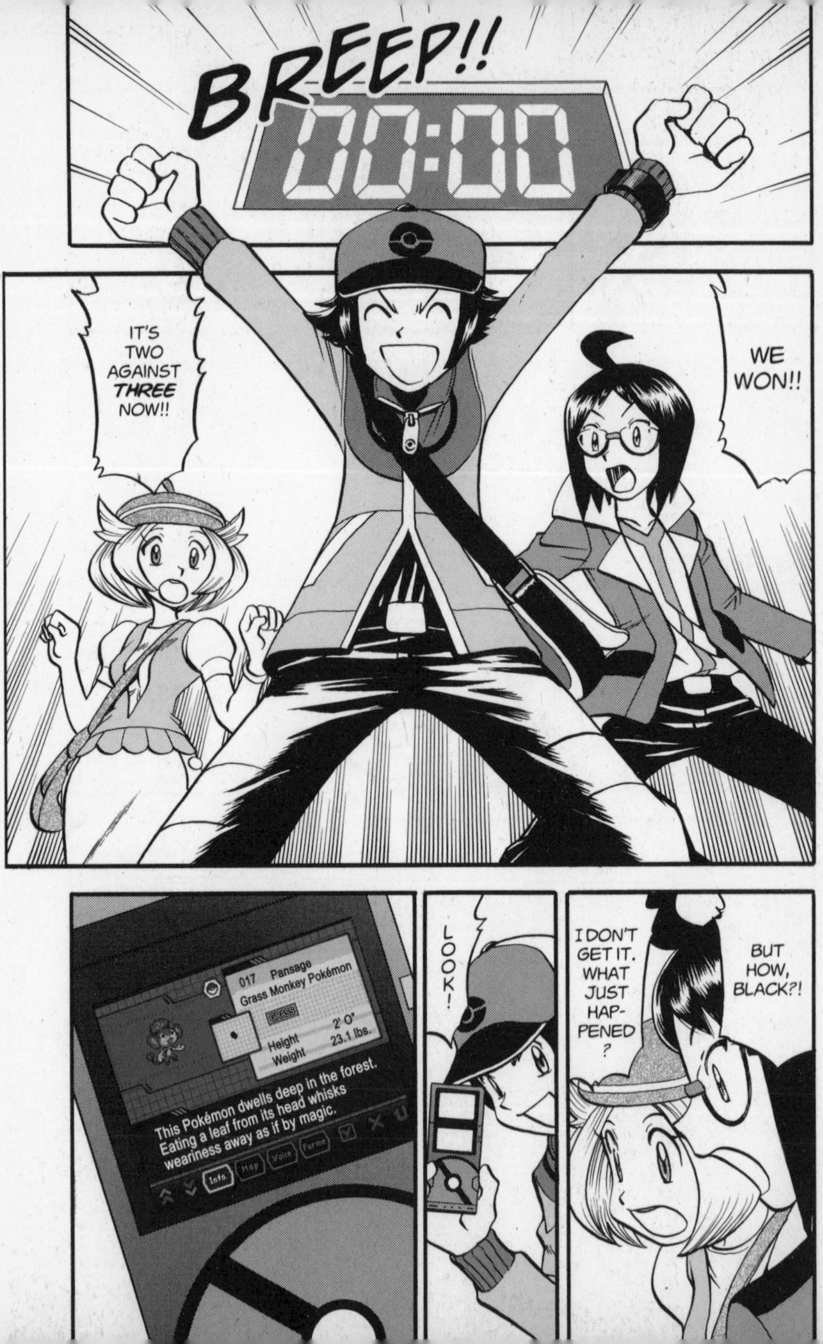

BREEP!!
00:00
IT'S TWO AGAINST THREE NOW!!
WE WON!!
017 Pansage
Grass Monkey Pokémon
GRASS
Height 2' 0"
Weight 23.1 lbs.
This Pokémon dwells deep in the forest. Eating a leaf from its head whisks weariness away as if by magic.
Info.
Map
Voice
Forms
LOOK!
I DON'T GET IT. WHAT JUST HAP-PENED?
BUT HOW, BLACK?!

mnch mnch

mnch mnch

mnch mnch

THEY FELL OFF PANSAGE'S HEAD DURING THE BATTLE...

THEY'RE EATING... PANSAGE'S LEAVES...

SHAAA!

SL UMP?..

SL...

EH?

SO IT'S TWO AGAINST *ZERO* AND—VICTORY!

AND PANSAGE AND PANPOUR ARE STILL GOING STRONG.

ALL THREE OF THEIR POKÉMON ARE DOWN.

TEPIG IS ON THE VERGE OF FAINTING. LOOKS LIKE WE'LL WIN EXACTLY WHEN THE TIME RUNS OUT.

THIR-TY SEC-ONDS LEFT.

WHAT ARE YOU DOING?

WHAK SMAK

OH MY.
TEPIG DECIDED
TO ATTACK
PANSAGE.
IT MUST KNOW IT
DOESN'T STAND
A CHANCE
AGAINST
PANPOUR.

WHUMP   THUMP

BUT
...

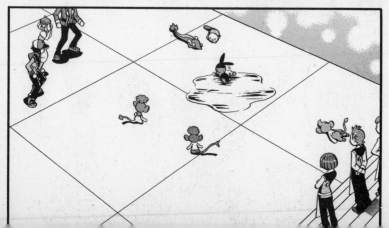

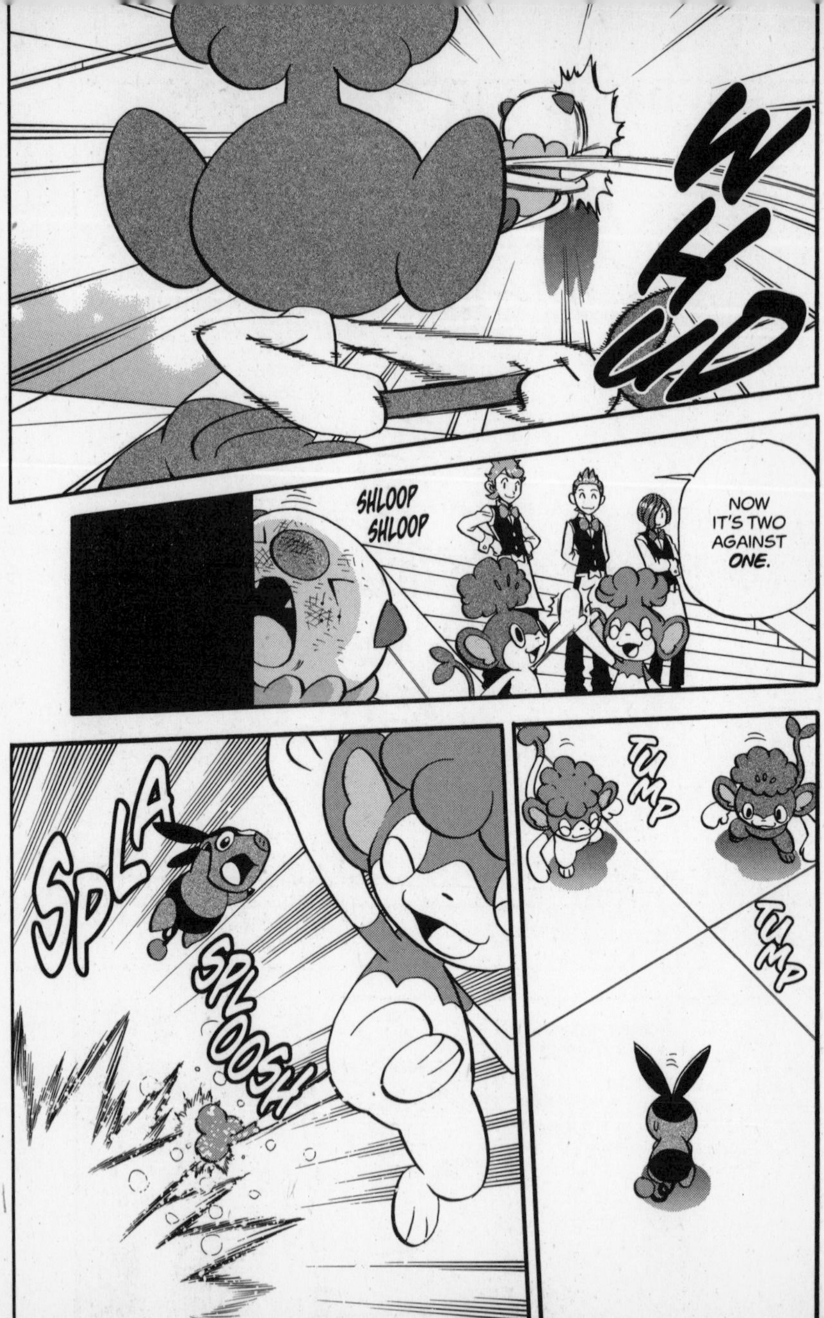
WHOMP
SHLOOP SHLOOP
NOW IT'S TWO AGAINST ONE.
SPLA
SPLOOSH
TUMP
TUMP

NOW ITS EVEN AGAIN, TWO AGAINST *TWO*!

BIANCA SAVED THE DAY!

Y-YOU'RE AMAZ-ING, BIANCA!

KA-KRAK

NOW THAT WE'VE SEEN IT...

BUT YOU CAN ONLY USE THAT TRICK ONCE!

Z WISH

IT'LL GROW OUT AGAIN— BUT NOT BEFORE THIS BATTLE IS OVER!

`05:23`

I'VE HEARD AN OSHAWOTT'S SCALCHOP IS LIKE A PERSON'S FINGERNAIL...

IT SMASH-ED OSHA-WOTT'S SCAL-CHOP!

THAT REALLY STEAMS ME UP!

APPARENTLY THAT HAS A POWERFUL EFFECT ON A FIRE-TYPE POKÉMON LIKE PANSEAR.

AN ATTACK USING OSHAWOTT'S SCALCHOP SOAKED IN WATER.

HUR-RAY!!

OSHAWOTT DEFENDED AGAINST THE ATTACK USING ITS SCAL-CHOP?!

GR R

GR R

Ee! Oo!

KA-POP

FLING

I'VE GOT IT!

OH, OH!

UM...

FINE, BLACK. BUT WHAT'S YOUR STRATEGY?

OSHA-WOTT, CHARGE!

THERE'S SOMETHING I'VE ALWAYS WANTED TO TRY...!

BIANCA! NOT AGAIN...!

SPLOO

AGH! NO...!

WHUMP

...AND WE FOUGHT A **TRIPLE BATTLE.**

I FOUGHT A TRAINER, A HIKER NAMED ANDY, ON MY WAY HERE...

THE THREE OF US ARE BASICALLY STANDING IN A ROW AND FIGHTING THREE SINGLE BATTLES *SEPARATELY...*

IN THAT BATTLE STYLE, A TRAINER USES THREE POKÉMON. THIS BATTLE IS JUST LIKE THAT...EXCEPT FOR ONE LITTLE THING.

SO THAT WOULD MAKE THIS BATTLE...

YOU CERTAINLY STUDY HARD!

OUR OPPONENT JUST NEEDS TO BE *IN RANGE* OF OUR ATTACK!

JUST LIKE IN A TRIPLE BATTLE, THE POKÉMON WE'RE ATTACKING DON'T NECESSARILY HAVE TO BE DIRECTLY IN *FRONT* OF US...

IF WE WERE TO GIVE IT A NAME, THAT IS.

...A TRIO BATTLE!!

IT'S PRETTY MUCH THREE AGAINST **TWO** NOW. AND **OUR** POKÉMON ARE STILL FULL OF VIM AND VIGOR.

SNIVY IS CLOSE TO FAINTING. I DON'T THINK IT CAN GET UP ANYMORE.

SNIVY!

AFTER ALL, WE RUN A THREE-STAR RESTAU-RANT!

WE, TOO, ARE THREE BRIGHT SHINING STARS.

OUR TEAM-WORK SPARKLES!

THIS BATTLE IS TOO UNCON-VENTIONAL FOR MY TASTE!

RELAX, CHE-REN...

LET'S SEE IF YOU CAN PUT OUT EVEN **ONE** OF OUR SHINING STARS.

NOW FOR A REALLY POWERFUL ATTACK...

YOU CAN NEITHER DODGE NOR WITHSTAND IT.

EX-ACT-LY.

IT'S THAT KIND OF MOVE, BIANCA.

YIKES! ALL THREE OF THEM GOT STRONGER ALL OF A SUDDEN!

TAKE THAT!!

KRESH

KRA SH

AH! LOOKS LIKE THEIR TEAMWORK IS IMPROVING.

WORKING TOGETHER TO SOLVE THOSE TESTS MUST HAVE TAUGHT THEM HOW TO COOPERATE BETTER.

BUT...

WORK-ING TOGETHER IS...

...WE'RE TRIPLETS.

...WHEN IT COMES TO COOPERATION...

...SECOND—NO, THIRD—NATURE FOR US!! NOW... WORK UP!

RAH

RAHRAHRAH

VWAP

TAKE THAT!

THEIR POKÉMON HAVE THE ADVANTAGE, BUT THAT DOESN'T MEAN OUR ATTACKS ARE POWER-LESS.

THAT'S RIGHT!

FWOP

pfp
pfp
pfp

NO WAY ARE WE GOING TO LOSE!

...WE COULD STILL WIN! IT WILL JUST TAKE LONGER!

THEN...

...AND WE'RE CAREFUL NOT TO SUSTAIN TOO MUCH DAMAGE FROM OUR OPPO-NENT'S AT-TACKS...

IF WE KEEP ATTACK-ING...

THAT'S THE SPIRIT, CHEREN!

PAT

I JUST WANTED TO UNDER-STAND YOUR STRATEGY, THAT'S ALL.

NO ONE'S WHINING ABOUT NOTHING.

CHEREN! BIANCA! READY...?

THIS BATTLE IS GOING TO BE ABOUT DEALING WITH THE DISADVANTAGE OF FIGHTING POKÉMON TYPES WHO HAVE AN ADVANTAGE OVER *OUR* POKÉMON TYPES.

EVEN THOUGH POOR OSHAWOTT'S UP AGAINST A POKÉ-MON WHO IT'S WEAK AGAINST...

READY! OSHAWOTT AND I WILL DO OUR BEST!

ISN'T THAT OBVI-OUS...?

HOW DID YOU GUYS DECIDE WHICH ORDER TO STAND IN?

WE'RE AT A DIS-ADVAN-TAGE!

WATER-TYPE PANPOUR AGAINST FIRE-TYPE TEPIG... GRASS-TYPE PANSAGE AGAINST WATER-TYPE OSHAWOTT... FIRE-TYPE PANSEAR AGAINST GRASS-TYPE SNIVY...

IT MIGHT SEEM LIKE WE HAVE AN UNFAIR ADVANTAGE... BUT PLEASE UNDERSTAND— THAT'S THE KIND OF GYM WE ARE.

WE POSITIONED OURSELVES BASED ON OUR KNOWLEDGE OF YOUR POKÉMON.

YOU GOT A PROBLEM WITH THAT...?!

OH, ONE MORE THING... YOU'RE NOT ALLOWED TO SWITCH PLACES DURING THIS BATTLE.

THAT'S OUR GYM'S *RAISON D'ETRE*!

THERE ARE MANY KINDS OF GYMS. OURS IS DEDICATED TO TEACH-ING OUR CHALLENG-ERS ABOUT POKÉMON *TYPES!*

AND IT'S ALL OVER!!

...INCIN- ERATE!

AH, SO THAT'S YOUR STRATEGY, IS IT? FINE. THEN PANSEAR...

krackle

THE WAY WE'RE LINED UP... THEY CAN ATTACK OUR POKÉMON WITH THE MOST EFFECTIVE MOVES.

HA HA... THEY'RE PRETTY TOUGH.

OSHAWOTT! USE WATER GUN TOO!

SPOO

SPLOOSH

PAN-POUR, WATER GUN!

WELL THEN... PANSAGE, VINE WHIP!

WAP WAP

ZWPPP

SNIVY...

...WRAP!!

SPROING

WHOMP

WHACK

IT'S THREE AGAINST THREE, SO TECHNICALLY WE'RE EVENLY MATCHED... BUT SO FAR...

THE TEAM WITH THE MOST POKÉMON STANDING AFTER THIRTY MINUTES WINS.

PLUS... THERE'S A THIRTY-MINUTE TIME LIMIT!

29:4

TODAY'S GYM BATTLE IS A THREE AGAINST THREE SPECIAL BATTLE! EACH COMPETITOR CAN ONLY USE *ONE* POKÉMON— MAKING IT UNLIKE MOST POKÉMON BATTLES.

IT'S NO USE!

WAPA

FOOSH!

TEP!

WHAP

THOK

CHALLENG-
ING THE
TRIPLET
GYM
LEADERS
ARE...

THE
STRIATON
GYM BATTLE
HAS BEGUN!

...WE
THREE
CHILDHOOD
FRIENDS!

Adventure ⑩ Their First Gym Battle

...WHO USE GRASS-TYPE, WATER-TYPE AND FIRE-TYPE POKÉMON...!

TRIPLET GYM LEADERS...

I'M BIANCA.

BLACK.

CHEREN.

AND WHAT ARE YOUR NAMES?

TIME FOR THE MAIN COURSE, A THREE AGAINST THREE GYM BATTLE!!

LET'S BEGIN !!

WE MIGHT HAVE A CHANCE AT WINNING AFTER ALL...!

THEY'RE TRYING OUT DIFFERENT MOVES TO HELP US FIGURE OUT THE ANSWERS TO THE TEST.

AND OUR POKÉMON ARE COOPERATING WITH EACH OTHER.

HUR-RAY!

FWAPPA!!

THIS!!

THE ANSWER IS...

DON'T WORRY. I KNOW WHAT THE NEXT ANSWER IS.

WE'LL INTRO-DUCE OUR-SELVES ONCE MORE.

YOU MADE IT!

CHILI.

CRESS.

CIL-AN.

WE'RE THE GYM LEADERS OF STRIA-TON GYM!

BLACK'S
CO-
OPERATING
WITH
BIANCA.

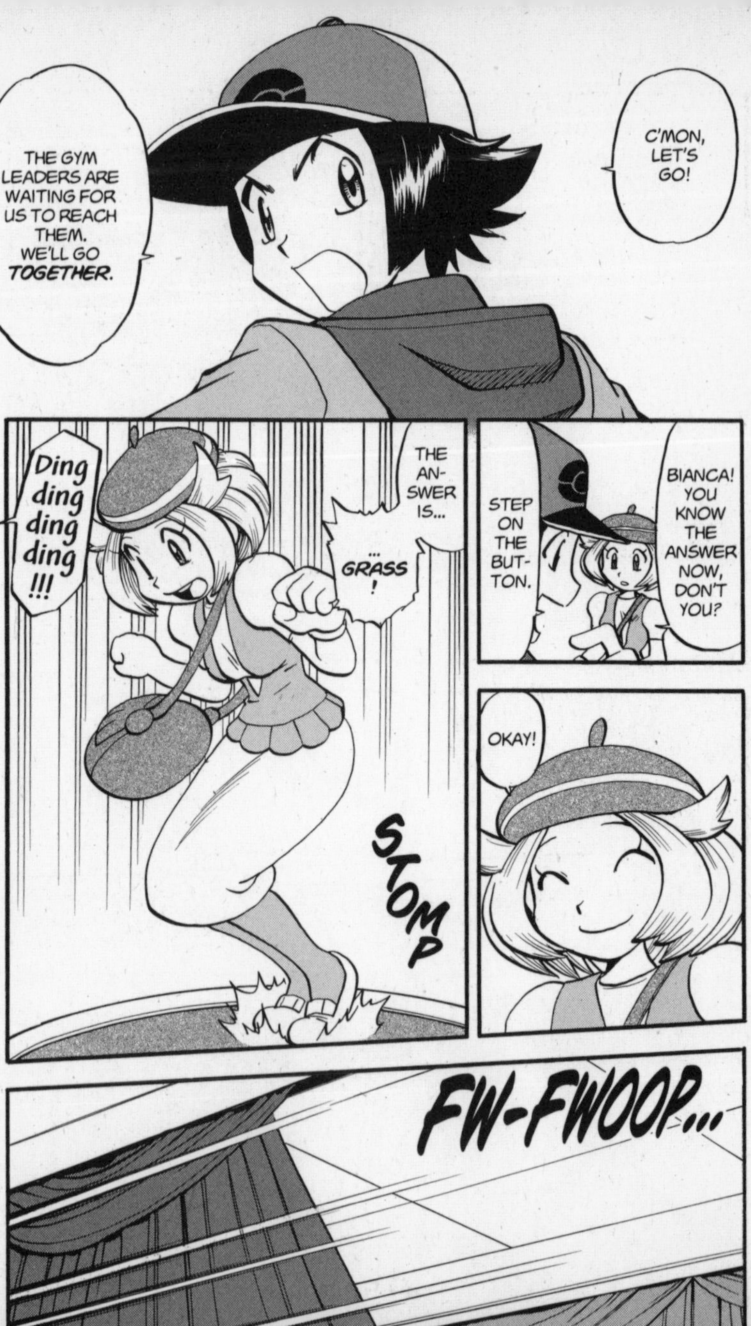

THE GYM LEADERS ARE WAITING FOR US TO REACH THEM. WE'LL GO *TOGETHER*.
C'MON, LET'S GO!
BIANCA! YOU KNOW THE ANSWER NOW, DON'T YOU?
STEP ON THE BUT-TON.
OKAY!
THE AN-SWER IS...
... *GRASS*!
Ding ding ding ding !!!
STOMP
FW-FWOOP...

TEP... EMBER!

HUH? O... OKAY.

WATCH HOW TEP AND SNIVY'S ATTACKS WORK AGAINST OSHAWOTT.

UH-HUH. I GUESS SO.

SEE? IT'S OKAY, RIGHT?

FOOSH!!

NOW DO YOU GET IT?

OH, DEAR! HANG IN THERE, OSHA-WOTT!

VINE WHIP!

SWAP

NEXT UP—SNIVY.

SINCE WATER IS A SOURCE OF NUTRITION FOR GRASS... IMAGINE THE GRASS-TYPE POKÉMON SIPHONING OFF THE WATER-TYPE'S STRENGTH.

GRASS IS EFFECTIVE AGAINST WATER.

I GET IT, I GET IT!

DO... WHAT?

...WE'RE WILLING TO DO IT IF **ALL THREE OF YOU** GET HERE.

...POKÉ-MON BATTLE!

FIGHT A THREE AGAINST THREE...

...

SEE YA! I HOPE...

KLK

BIAN-CA!

WE AREN'T THAT STRICT. WE'D NEVER DISQUALIFY SOMEBODY OVER A TRIVIAL THING LIKE THAT. AHA HA HA!

AGH! I KNEW IT.

BONK!

JUST KIDDING!!

WHY DON'T YOU THREE TEAM UP? SHE CAN LEARN AS YOU GO ALONG.

SHE DOESN'T EVEN KNOW THE *BASICS*. SHE'S *HOPELESS*.

...DOESN'T HAVE A CLUE ABOUT POKÉMON TYPE COMPATIBILITY, DOES SHE?

BUT YOUR FRIEND...

SOO...

BUT...

OUR GYM RULE IS THAT YOU HAVE TO FIGHT *ONE* OF US AFTER YOU PASS ALL THE TESTS.

IT'S OKAY.

WAIT A MIN—

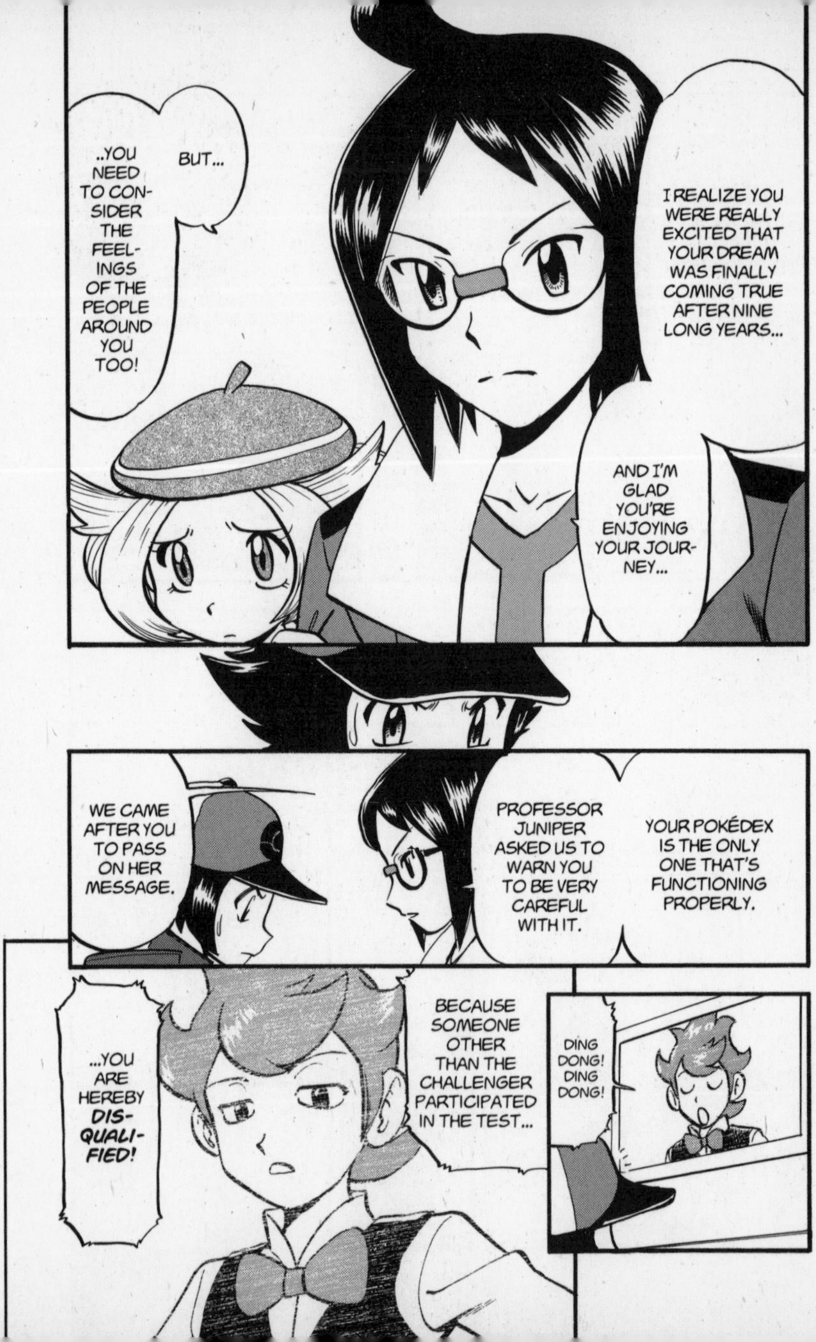

I REALIZE YOU WERE REALLY EXCITED THAT YOUR DREAM WAS FINALLY COMING TRUE AFTER NINE LONG YEARS...
AND I'M GLAD YOU'RE ENJOYING YOUR JOURNEY...
BUT...
..YOU NEED TO CONSIDER THE FEELINGS OF THE PEOPLE AROUND YOU TOO!
YOUR POKÉDEX IS THE ONLY ONE THAT'S FUNCTIONING PROPERLY.
PROFESSOR JUNIPER ASKED US TO WARN YOU TO BE VERY CAREFUL WITH IT.
WE CAME AFTER YOU TO PASS ON HER MESSAGE.
DING DONG! DING DONG!
BECAUSE SOMEONE OTHER THAN THE CHALLENGER PARTICIPATED IN THE TEST...
...YOU ARE HEREBY ***DISQUALIFIED!***

LET'S **OPEN** IT.

'ALL RIGHT'

I COULDN'T WAIT...

THE MORNING WE WERE GOING TO RECEIVE OUR POKÉMON, YOU RUSHED AHEAD AND OPENED THE BOX WITHOUT US, REMEMBER?!

OKAY. CLEARLY BIANCA IS AT LEAST PARTIALLY AT FAULT HERE... BUT DON'T **YOU** HAVE SOMETHING TO SAY TO US AS WELL...?

F-FOR REAL?

THEY BROKE! BOTH OF THEM! AND WE'RE STILL WAITING FOR THEM TO GET REPAIRED.

AND WHAT DO YOU THINK HAPPENED TO THE OTHER TWO POKÉDEXES THAT GOT DRENCHED IN THE CHAOS THAT ENSUED...?!

AND THAT'S HOW PRO-FESSOR JUNIPER'S LABORATORY GOT TRASHED...

TO TOP IT OFF, YOU DIDN'T EVEN **THANK** PROFESSOR JUNIPER FOR GIVING YOU THIS OPPORTUNITY! AND THEN YOU TOOK OFF WITHOUT SAYING GOODBYE TO ANY OF US!

YOU WEREN'T THE ONLY ONE LOOKING FORWARD TO SETTING OUT ON YOUR JOURNEY WITH YOUR POKÉDEX! BUT THANKS TO YOU, WE WEREN'T ABLE TO START ON TIME!

ER...

UH...

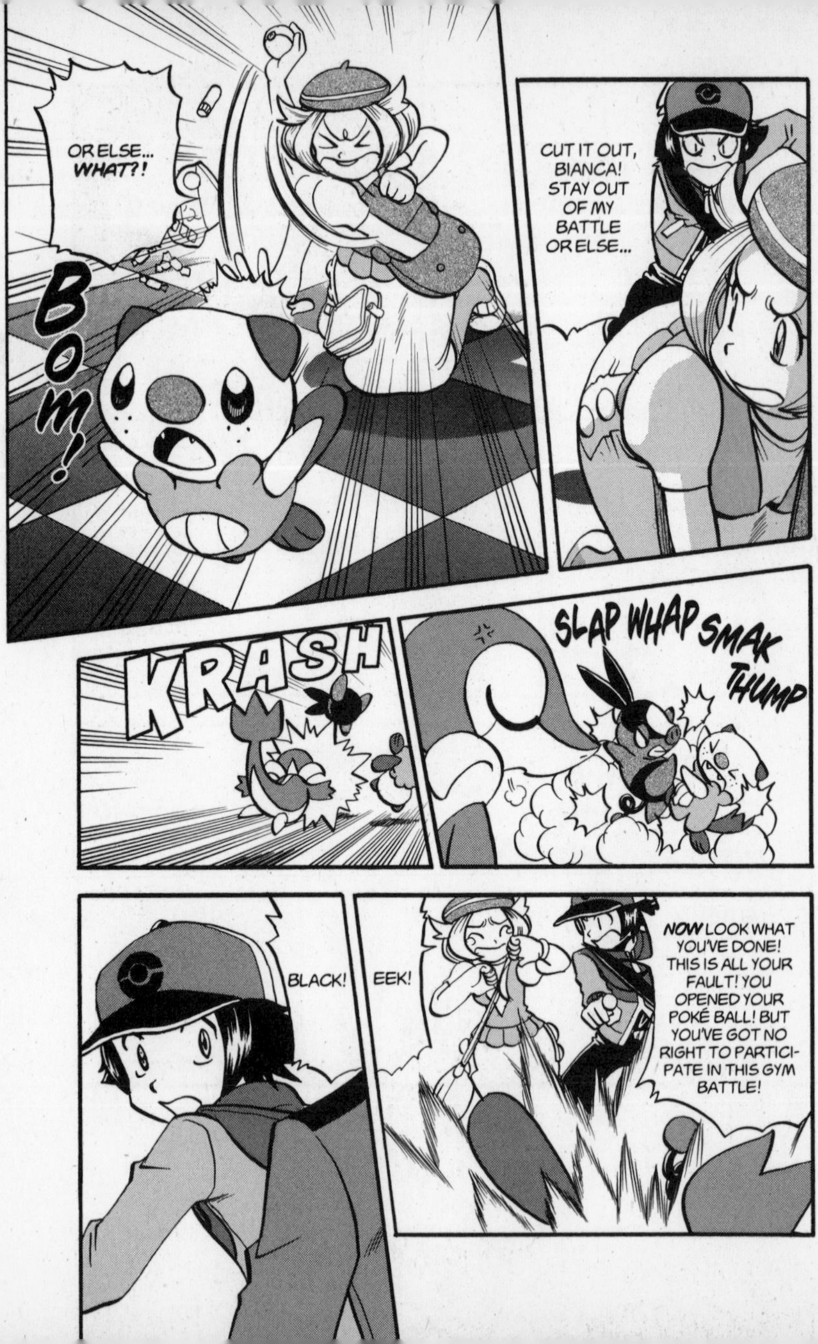
CUT IT OUT, BIANCA! STAY OUT OF MY BATTLE OR ELSE...
OR ELSE... WHAT?!
BOM!
SLAP WHAP SMAK THUMP
KRASH
NOW LOOK WHAT YOU'VE DONE! THIS IS ALL YOUR FAULT! YOU OPENED YOUR POKÉ BALL! BUT YOU'VE GOT NO RIGHT TO PARTICI-PATE IN THIS GYM BATTLE!
EEK!
BLACK!

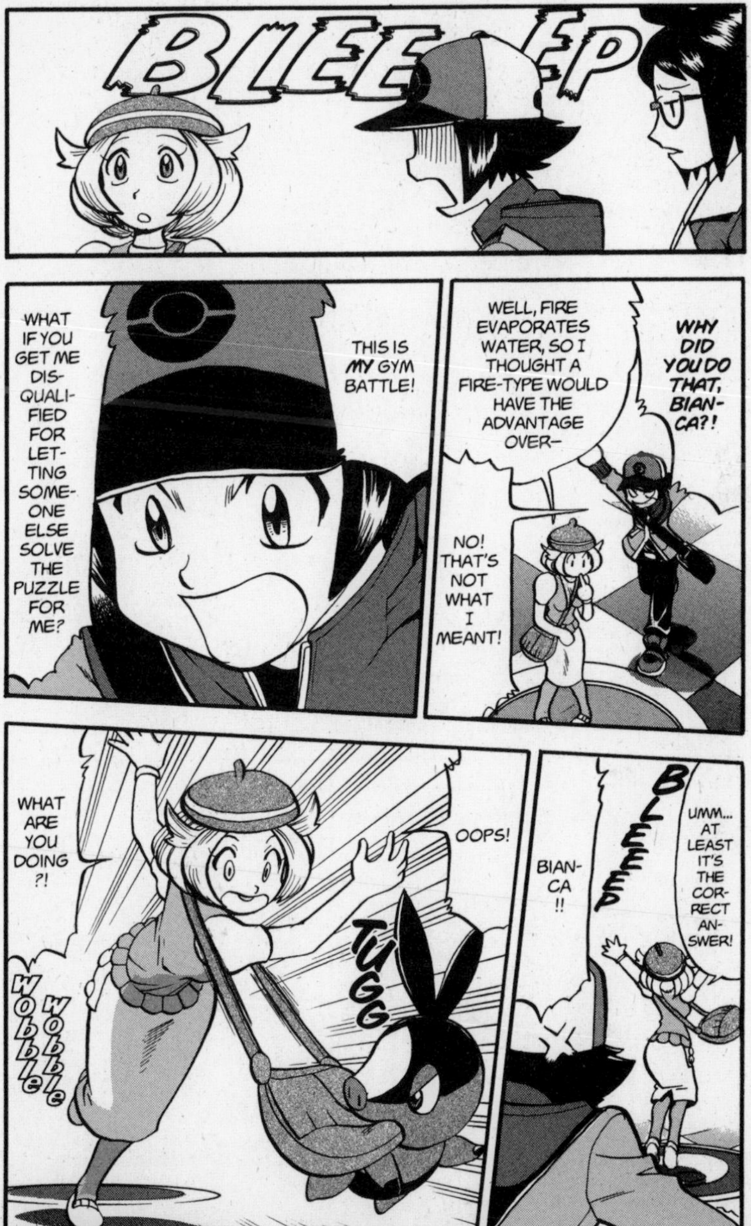
BLEEEEP
THIS IS MY GYM BATTLE!
WHAT IF YOU GET ME DIS-QUALI-FIED FOR LET-TING SOME-ONE ELSE SOLVE THE PUZZLE FOR ME?
WHY DID YOU DO THAT, BIAN-CA?!
WELL, FIRE EVAPORATES WATER, SO I THOUGHT A FIRE-TYPE WOULD HAVE THE ADVANTAGE OVER—
NO! THAT'S NOT WHAT I MEANT!
UMM... AT LEAST IT'S THE COR-RECT AN-SWER!
BLEEEP
BIAN-CA!!
OOPS!
WHAT ARE YOU DOING?!
TUGG
Wobble wobble

...YOU HAVE TO PUSH THE BUTTON ON THE FLOOR THAT MATCHES THE POKÉMON TYPE WITH AN ADVANTAGE OVER THE POKÉMON TYPE ON THE CURTAIN. THAT'S HOW YOU GET TO THE NEXT STAGE OF THE CHALLENGE.

IN THIS GYM...

IF YOU MAKE IT THAT FAR.

THE MAIN COURSE WILL BE YOUR BATTLE AGAINST US.

WE'LL BE WAITING FOR YOU IN THE BACK.

Aghhh!

FIRE!

THE SYMBOL ON THE CURTAIN STANDS FOR WATER! THE POKÉMON TYPE THAT'S STRONGEST AGAINST WATER WOULD BE—

GOT IT!

THE TRIPLE LEADERS!!

THEY'RE *TRIP-LETS*!!

I'VE BEEN RESEARCHING ALL THE GYMS FOR AGES, YOU KNOW.

THAT'S THE TWIST AT THE STRIATON GYM.

CHOOSING THE POKÉMON TYPE THAT GIVES YOU AN ADVANTAGE OVER YOUR OPPONENT'S POKÉMON TYPE IS THE FIRST STEP TO VICTORY!

THAT'S VERY IMPORTANT.

CHOOSE THE *TYPE* OF POKÉMON FOR YOUR GYM BATTLE CAREFULLY.

I SUPPOSE YOU KNOW HOW TO GET PAST THE *APPETIZER* BEFORE YOU FIGHT US THEN...?

YOU CERTAINLY HAVE DONE YOUR HOMEWORK!

SH-
SHFF

STRIATON GYM! YEP!

G-GYM BATTLE...? YOU MEAN THIS RESTAURANT IS THE—

ALL OF THOSE THREE!

NOT **ONE** OF THOSE THREE!

AND ONE OF THOSE THREE IS THE GYM LEADER?

NOPE!

THE TEA SERVICE IS THE SIGNAL THAT THE FULL-COURSE SERVICE IS ABOUT TO START. IN OTHER WORDS...

W-WHY'S THAT, BLACK?

...THE TEA TO BE SERVED!

I'VE BEEN WAITING AND WAITING FOR...

IT'S THE SIGNAL FOR THE GYM BATTLE TO START!!

KLATTER

BINGO!

TUG!

PRE-CISELY!

A CUP FOR YOUR FRIENDS AS WELL.

I'VE NEVER DRUNK ANYTHING SO FLAVORFUL IN ALL MY LIFE!

IT'S DELICIOUS!

YAHOO!

THEIR MOVES ARE PERFECTLY SYNCHRONIZED!

OH! THAT'S SO COOL!

THE RED ONE MUST BE A FIRE-TYPE POKÉMON TRAINER.

AND THOSE FLAMES ARE DRAWING OUT THE BEST FLAVOR FROM THE TEA LEAVES.

HE CHOSE THE FRESHEST WATER TO BREW THE TEA.

THE BLUE ONE MUST BE A WATER-TYPE POKÉMON TRAINER.

HIS CHOICE OF TEA IS SUPERB.

THE GREEN ONE MUST BE A GRASS-TYPE POKÉMON TRAINER.

WE'D BETTER SHOW HIM SOME HOSPITALITY.

AFTER ALL, HE DID MAKE A RESERVATION FOR A **FULL-COURSE** SERVICE...

TAKE IT EASY...

BOM

BOm

BOm!!

BOm

OUR APOLOGIES FOR KEEPING YOU WAITING.

WE'D LIKE TO OFFER YOU SOME TEA BEFORE YOUR MEAL SERVICE BEGINS.

MR. BLACK ...?

krkl krkl

WH-WHO WAS W-WHAT...?

DON'T YOU "LONG TIME NO SEE" ME, BLACK! WHO WAS THAT GIRL?!

WHAT?!

SOMEHOW I ENDED UP WORKING FOR HER... AND NOW WE TRAVEL TOGETHER!

OH! THAT'S WHITE. SHE RUNS A TALENT AGENCY FOR POKÉMON. THEY PERFORM IN MOVIES AND TV COMMERCIALS AND STUFF LIKE THAT.

HUH? WHAT'S NOT TO GET?

ME NEITHER.

I DON'T GET IT. NOT ONE BIT.

LET'S TOSS HIM OUT.

THAT CUSTOMER WITH THE CAP HAS BEEN GETTING INTO A LOT OF ARGUMENTS WITH OUR PATRONS.

WEL-COME!

DON'T BE RIDICU-LOUS! WE'VE GOT TO TALK TO BLACK!

WHO IS THAT GIRL ANY-WAY?! LET'S FOLLOW HER, CHEREN!

THE FULL-COURSE MEALS ARE—

OUR SPECIALTY IS A RANGE OF DISHES ESPECIALLY TAILORED TO THE DISCRIMI-NATING POKÉMON TRAINER'S TASTE.

OH!

WE'RE JUST HERE TO SEE A FRIEND.

NO THANKS.

LONG TIME NO SEE!!

HEY! CHEREN! BIANCA!

OH! HE'S HAVING TEA WITH... A *GIRL!*

THERE'S BLACK!

I DON'T KNOW ABOUT THAT, BIANCA...

I CAN'T BELIEVE HIM! HE'S ON A *DATE!* HE HASN'T THE FOGGIEST IDEA HOW MUCH TROUBLE WE TOOK TO FIND HIM!

...A DATE TO ME.

DOESN'T LOOK LIKE...

BY ANY CHANCE, HAVE YOU SEEN A BOY WHO SHOUTS SLOGANS LIKE THAT?

"I AM SO TOTALLY ABSOLUTELY GONNA WIN THAT TOURNAMENT!!!"

"I'M GOING TO THE POKÉMON LEAGUE! AND I'M GONNA *WIN!!!*"

CAN I HELP YOU?

UM... EX-CUSE ME.

AS A MATTER OF FACT, I HAVE...

HE WAS WITH SOME POKÉMON. HE SHOUTED THOSE WORDS EXACTLY! AND THEN HE ENTERED THAT BUILDING OVER THERE.

HEY!

LOOKS LIKE A RESTAURANT...

WE'VE FINALLY CAUGHT UP TO HIM.

NO THANKS TO YOU, BIANCA...

GREAT! THANK YOU VERY MUCH, MA'AM!

I HAD NO IDEA YOU WERE SUCH A DAWDLER!

I KNOW YOU LIKE TO TAKE THINGS AT YOUR OWN PACE, BUT...

YES, YOU DID. LET'S MOVE ON, BIANCA.

CHEREN! I LOST! WAHHH...

WE HAVE TO WARN HIM TO TAKE EXTRA GOOD CARE OF HIS POKÉDEX— BECAUSE IT'S THE ONLY ONE THAT'S STILL WORKING.

COME ON! WE HAVE TO CATCH UP TO BLACK AS SOON AS POSSIBLE.

CHEREN, LOOK!

OH!

BUT YOU KEEP GETTING SIDE-TRACKED! WE DON'T HAVE TIME TO STOP AND BATTLE EVERY WILD POKÉMON WE RUN INTO! WE'VE GOT A JOB TO DO!

WE'VE REACHED STRIATON CITY. LET'S GO! HURRY UP!

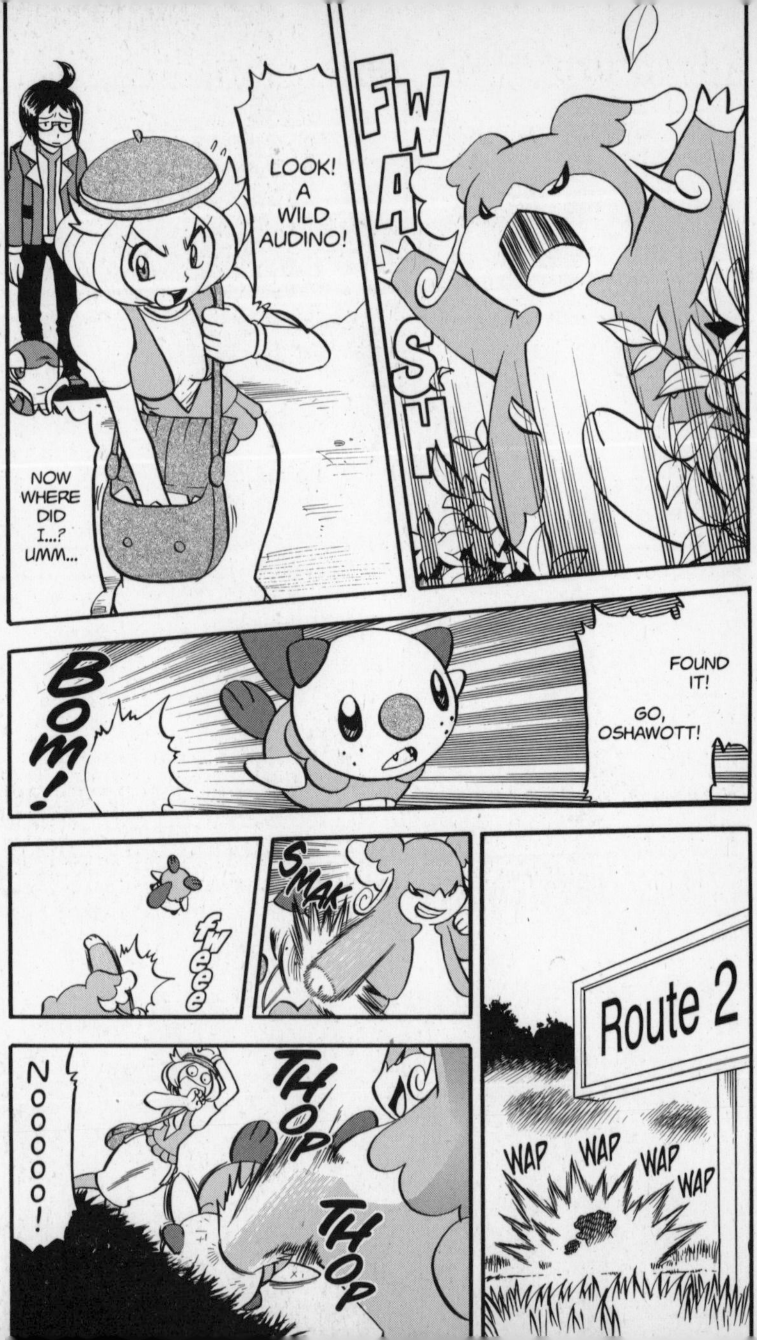

LOOK! A WILD AUDINO!
FWASH
NOW WHERE DID I...? UMM...
FOUND IT!
GO, OSHAWOTT!
BOOM!
fweee
SMAK
Route 2
WAP WAP WAP WAP
THOP THOP THOP
NOOOOOO!

Adventure ⑨ Welcome to Striaton City!!

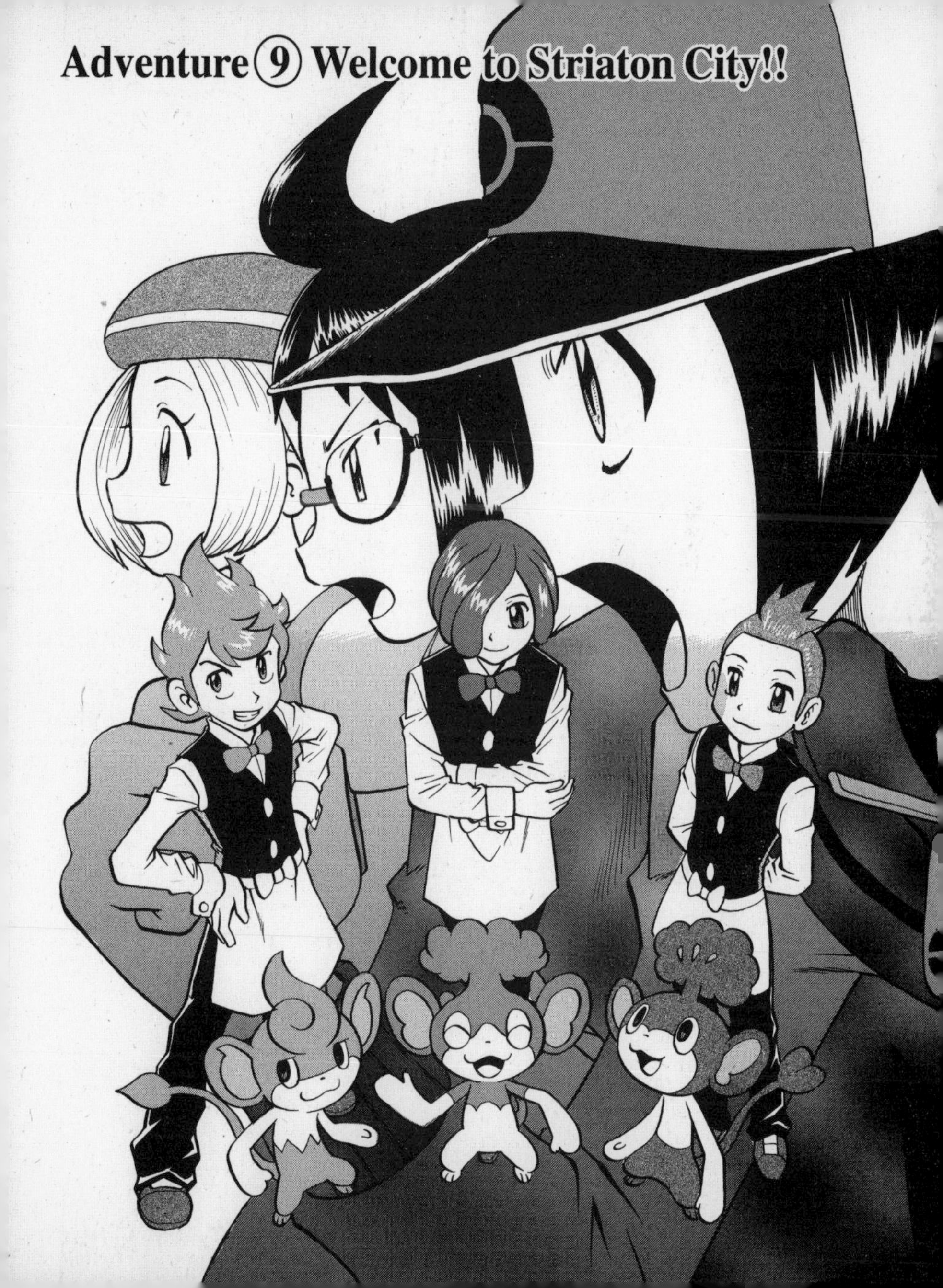

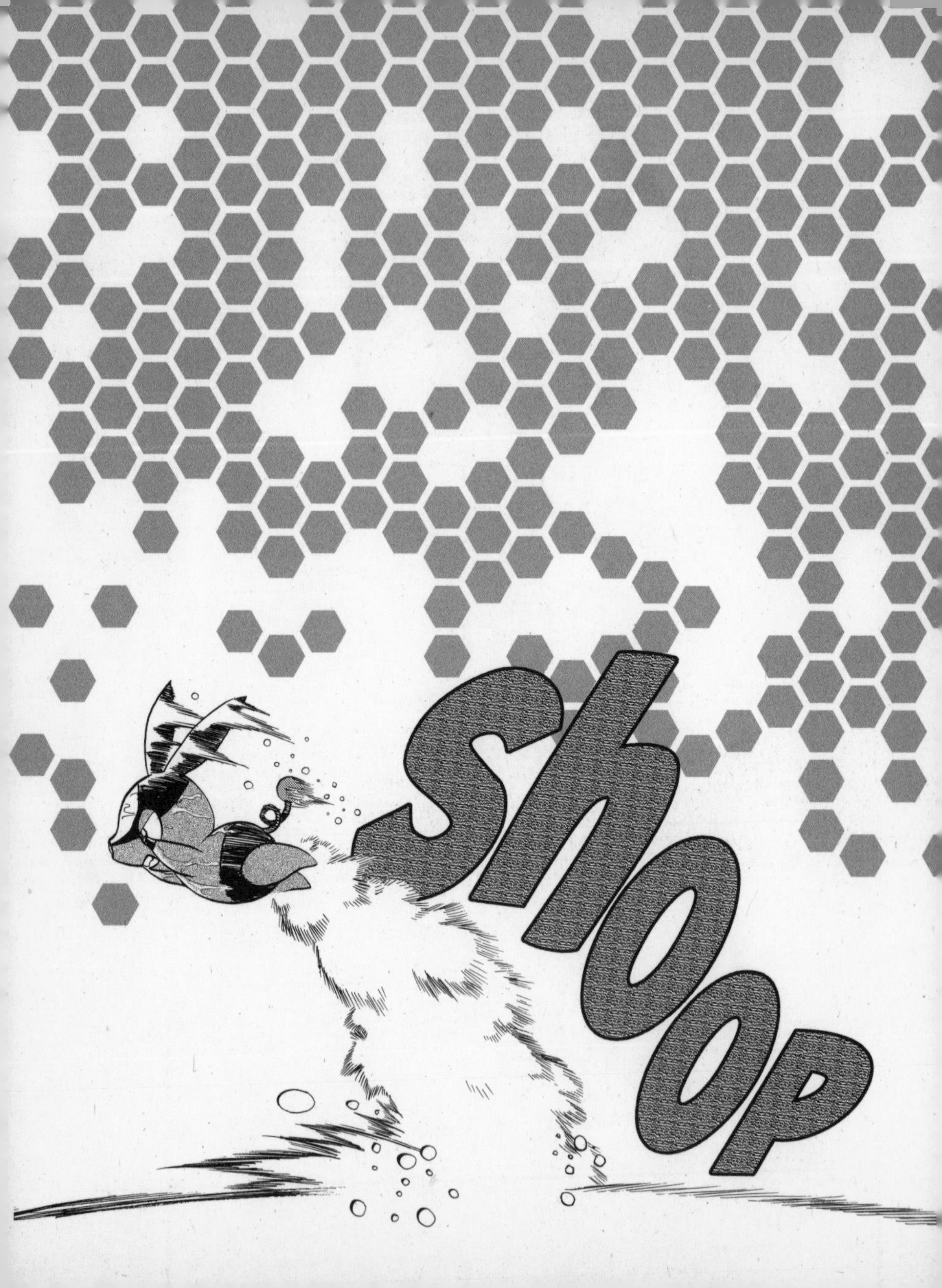
SHOOOP

...OF A SIMPLER TIME AND PLACE.

IT WAS A VERY PEACEFUL HAPPY DREAM...

N WAS REALLY LITTLE, AND HE WAS WITH HIS POKÉMON.

...HE'S STILL A GOOD GUY AT HEART.

BUT...

HE MIGHT SEE THINGS DIFFERENTLY FROM US...

I DON'T KNOW...

I'M NOT SURE N IS ALL BAD, WHITE.

NOT ONLY DO THEY MAKE STUPID SPEECHES— THEY ATTACK INNOCENT PEOPLE!

WHAT A ROTTEN BUNCH!

...I HAP-PENED TO SEE AN IMAGE FROM N'S DREAM.

...MUSHA ATE A PART OF...

...N'S DREAM.

WHEN TEP KNOCKED HIM DOWN, HE FELL NEAR MUSHA AND...

IN THE FOG MUSHA EXHALED...

AFTER EATING SOMEBODY'S DREAM, MUSHA BREATHES SOME OF IT OUT THROUGH THE NOSE.

BOM BOM BOM

HAVE A NICE REST.

HERE'S A POTION FOR YOU. AND AN ORAN BERRY TOO.

AND GALVAN-TULA TOO. THANKS A LOT, EVERY-ONE.

BOM

...SOUNDED AWFULLY SIMILAR...

HEY, BLACK... DID YOU NOTICE THAT THE THINGS N WAS TALKING ABOUT...

...

MAYBE HE'S ONE OF THEM!

...TO WHAT TEAM PLASMA WAS SAYING?

...PUZZLE I CANNOT SOLVE.

I'VE COME ACROSS YET ANOTHER...

HIS POKÉMON FAINTED, BUT HE STILL WON'T USE A POKÉ BALL?!

MUSHA!

BRAV!

TEP!

I NEVER IMAGINED A POKÉMON MIGHT FEEL THAT WAY...

I WAS ABLE TO HEAR YOUR TEPIG'S VOICE.

Wheez.

Wheez.

H...HEY! WAIT!

IT'S ALL RIGHT. LET'S GO.

GURDURR, PURRLOIN, PIDOVE— YOU FOUGHT WELL.

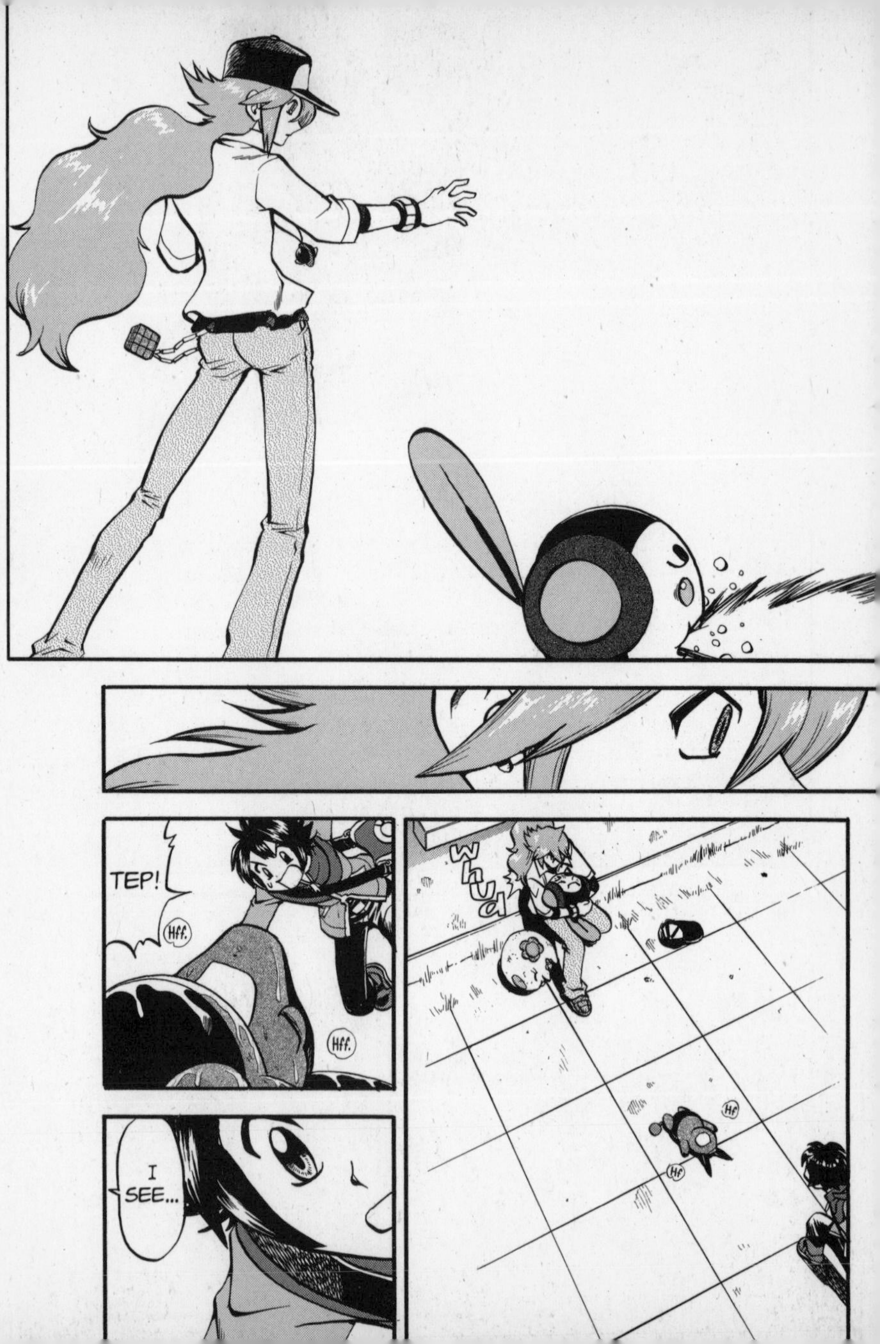
WHUD
TEP!
Hff.
Hff.
Hf
Hf
I SEE...

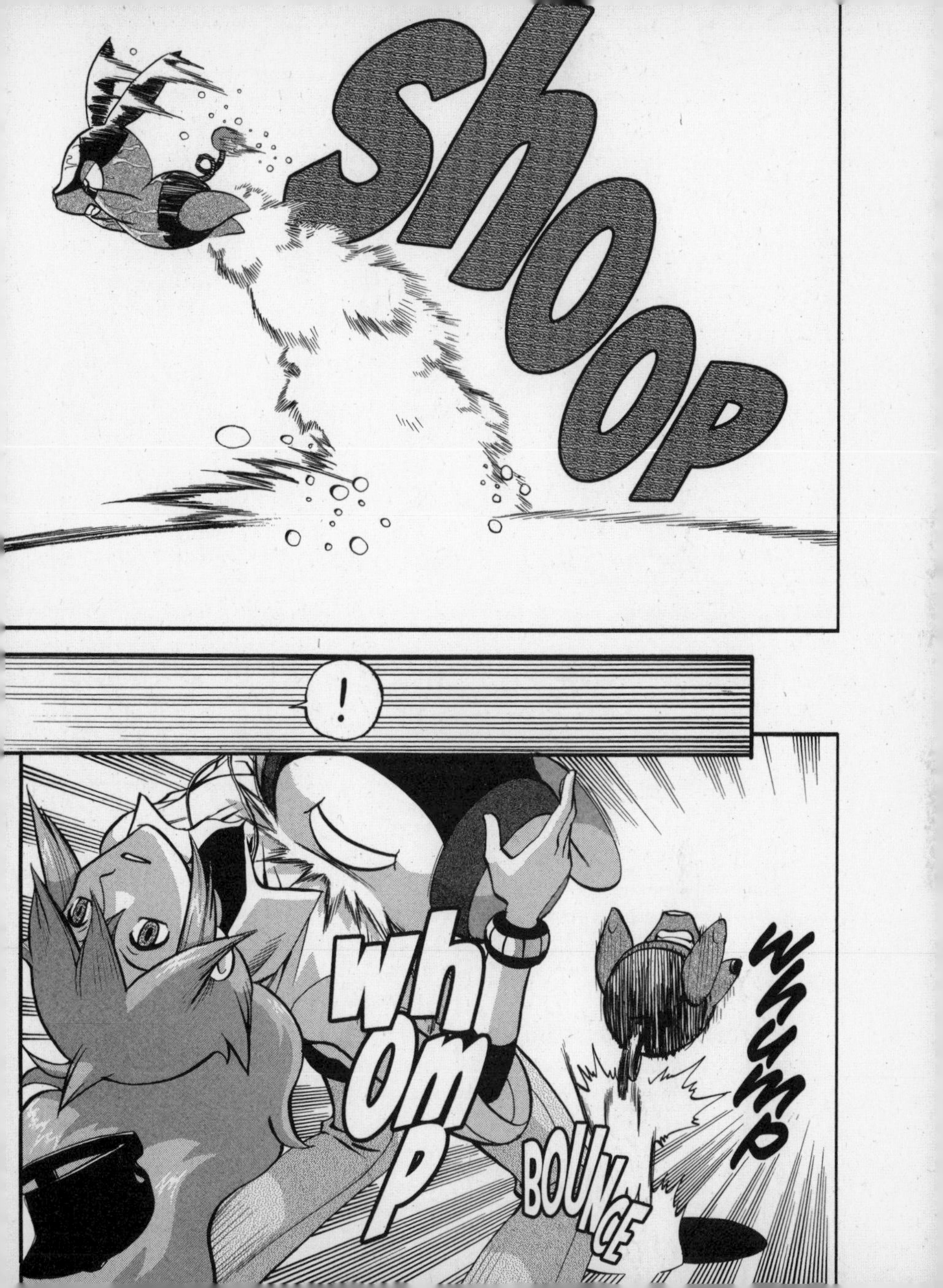
SHOOOP
!
WHUMP
whomp
BOUNCE

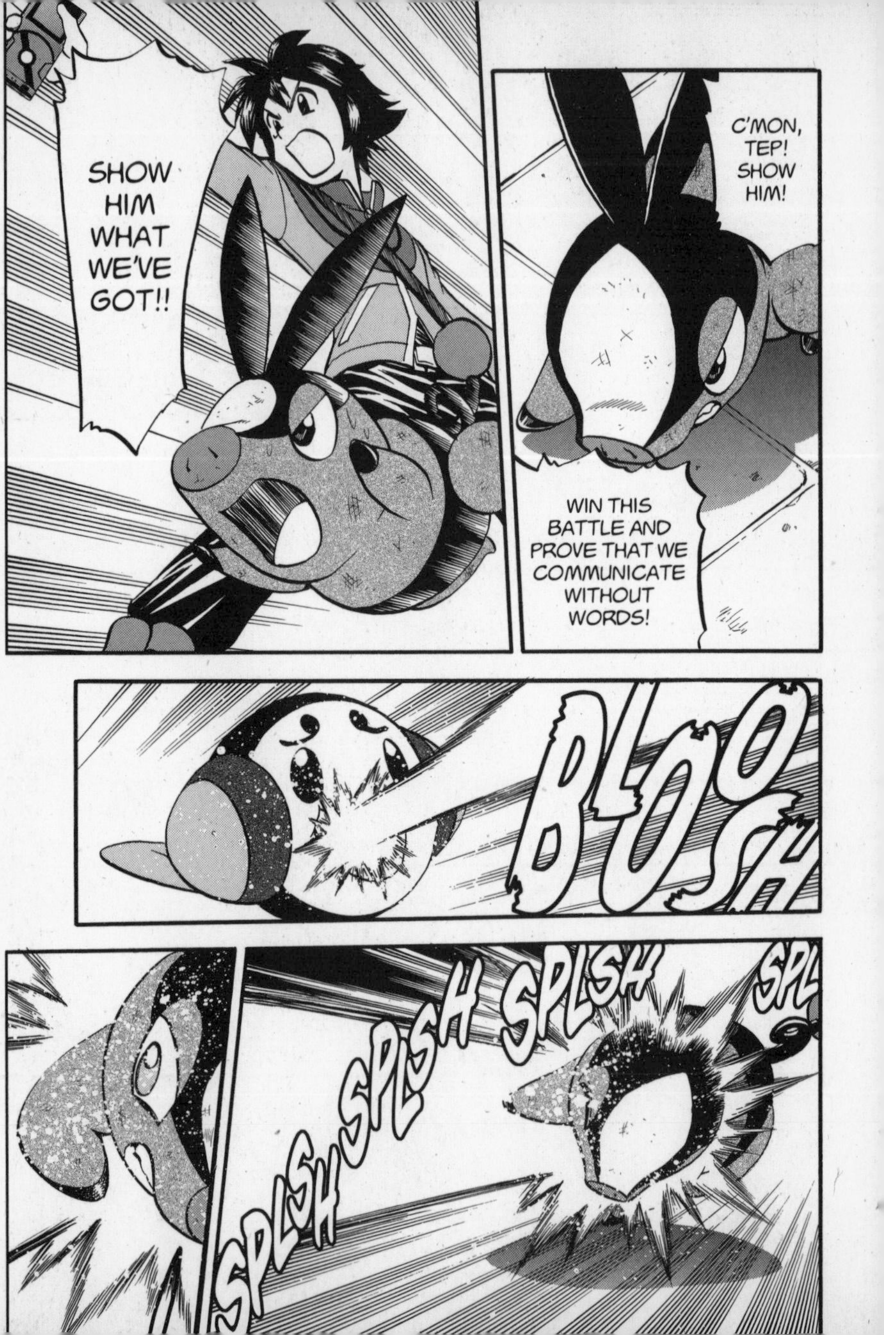
SHOW HIM WHAT WE'VE GOT!!
C'MON, TEP! SHOW HIM!
WIN THIS BATTLE AND PROVE THAT WE COMMUNICATE WITHOUT WORDS!
BLOOOSH
SPLSH SPLSH SPLSH SPLSH
SPL

IT'S NATURAL FOR PEOPLE TO WANT TO LEARN MORE ABOUT POKÉMON BECAUSE WE *LIKE THEM SO MUCH!*

AS FOR THE POKÉ-DEX...

I'M PROUD OF THAT.

A FAMOUS PROFESSOR ENTRUSTED ME WITH IT ON MY JOURNEY.

THIS TOOL WAS INVENTED SO WE COULD LEARN MORE ABOUT THEM.

...THE REST OF US NEED A POKÉDEX AND POKÉ BALLS. THAT'S HOW WE UNDER-STAND EACH OTHER!

THAT'S WHY...

YOU'RE RIGHT ABOUT ONE THING. I CAN'T HEAR THESE POKÉMON VOICES YOU KEEP TALKING ABOUT.

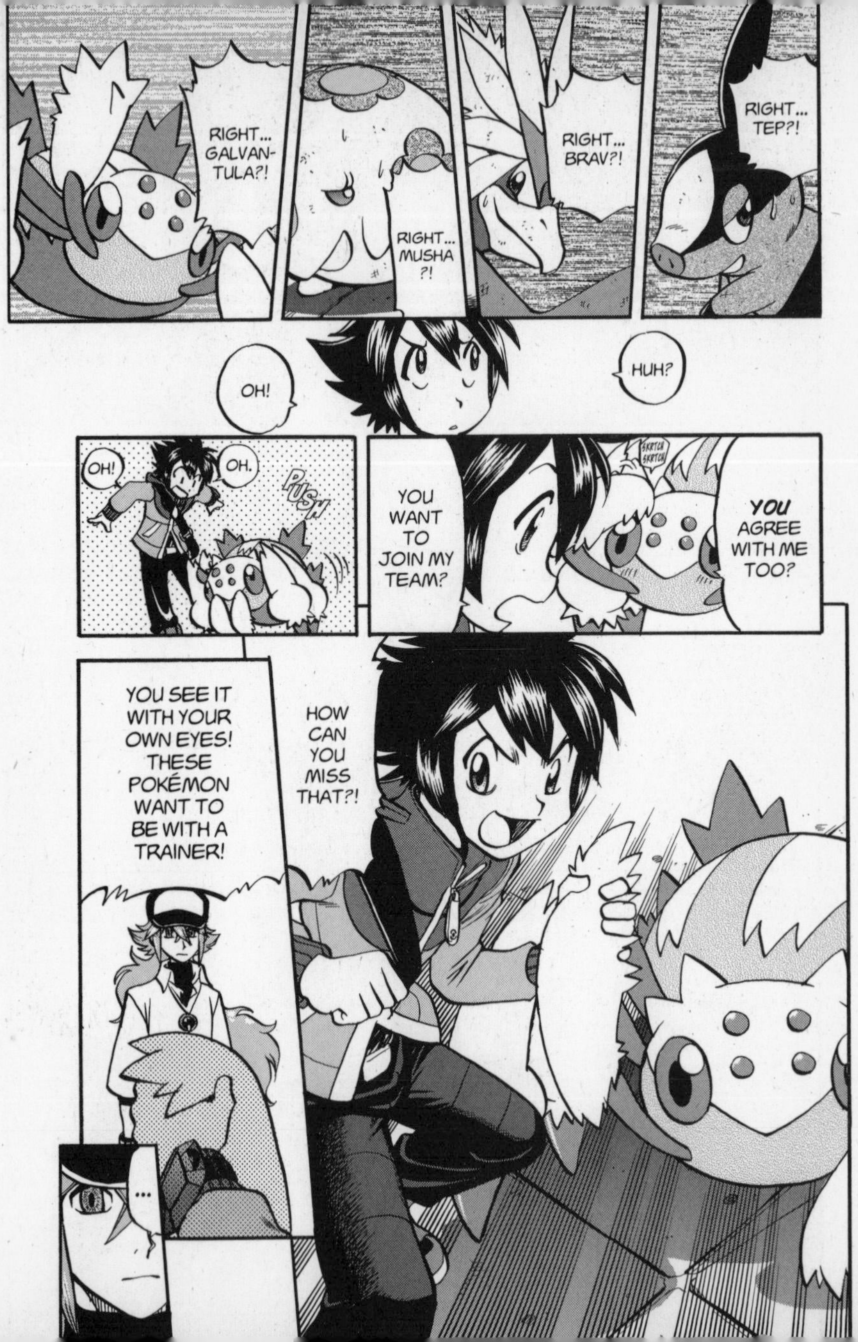
RIGHT... TEP?!
RIGHT... BRAV?!
RIGHT... MUSHA ?!
RIGHT... GALVAN-TULA?!
HUH?
OH!
SKRTCH SKRTCH
YOU AGREE WITH ME TOO?
YOU WANT TO JOIN MY TEAM?
OH.
OH!
PUSH
HOW CAN YOU MISS THAT?!
YOU SEE IT WITH YOUR OWN EYES! THESE POKÉMON WANT TO BE WITH A TRAINER!
...

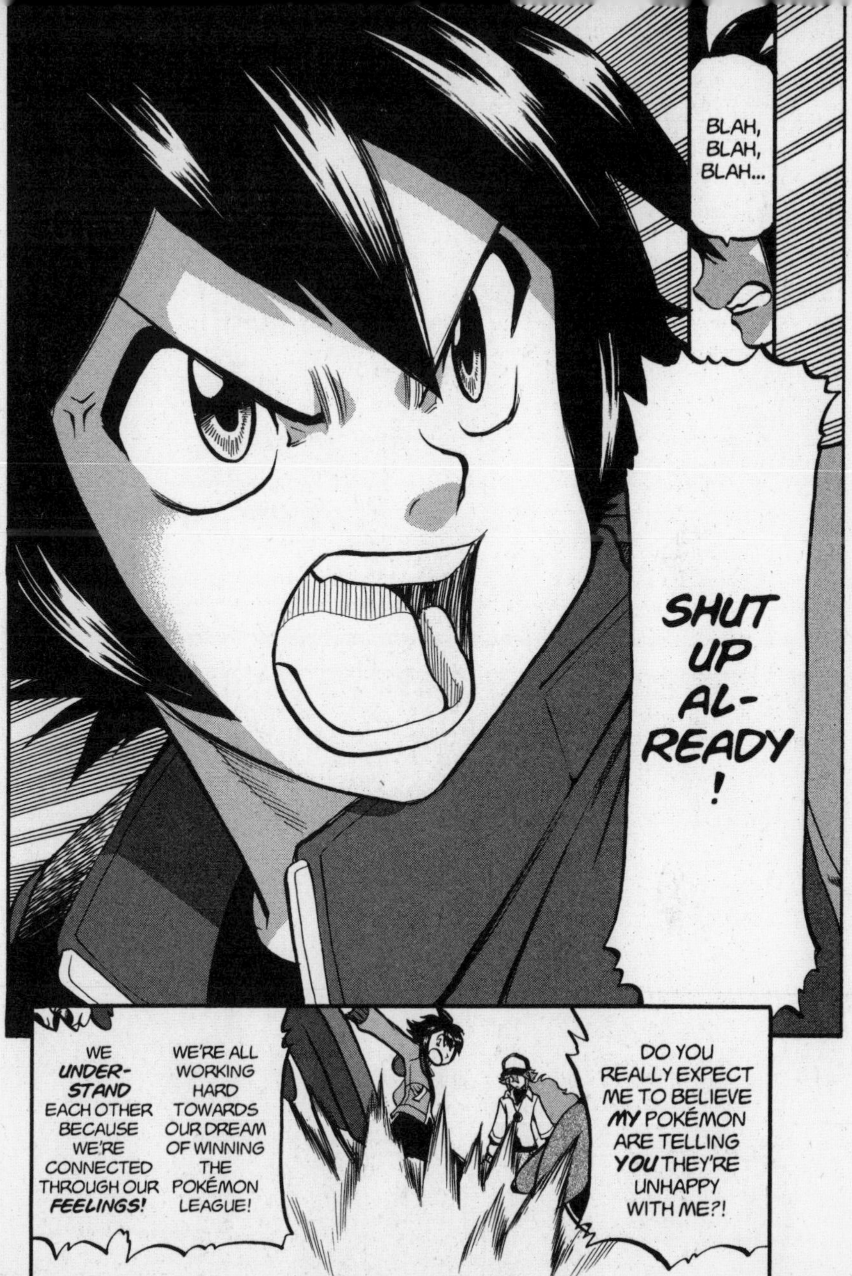
BLAH, BLAH, BLAH...
SHUT UP AL-READY!
DO YOU REALLY EXPECT ME TO BELIEVE *MY* POKÉMON ARE TELLING *YOU* THEY'RE UNHAPPY WITH ME?!
WE'RE ALL WORKING HARD TOWARDS OUR DREAM OF WINNING THE POKÉMON LEAGUE!
WE *UNDER-STAND* EACH OTHER BECAUSE WE'RE CONNECTED THROUGH OUR *FEELINGS!*

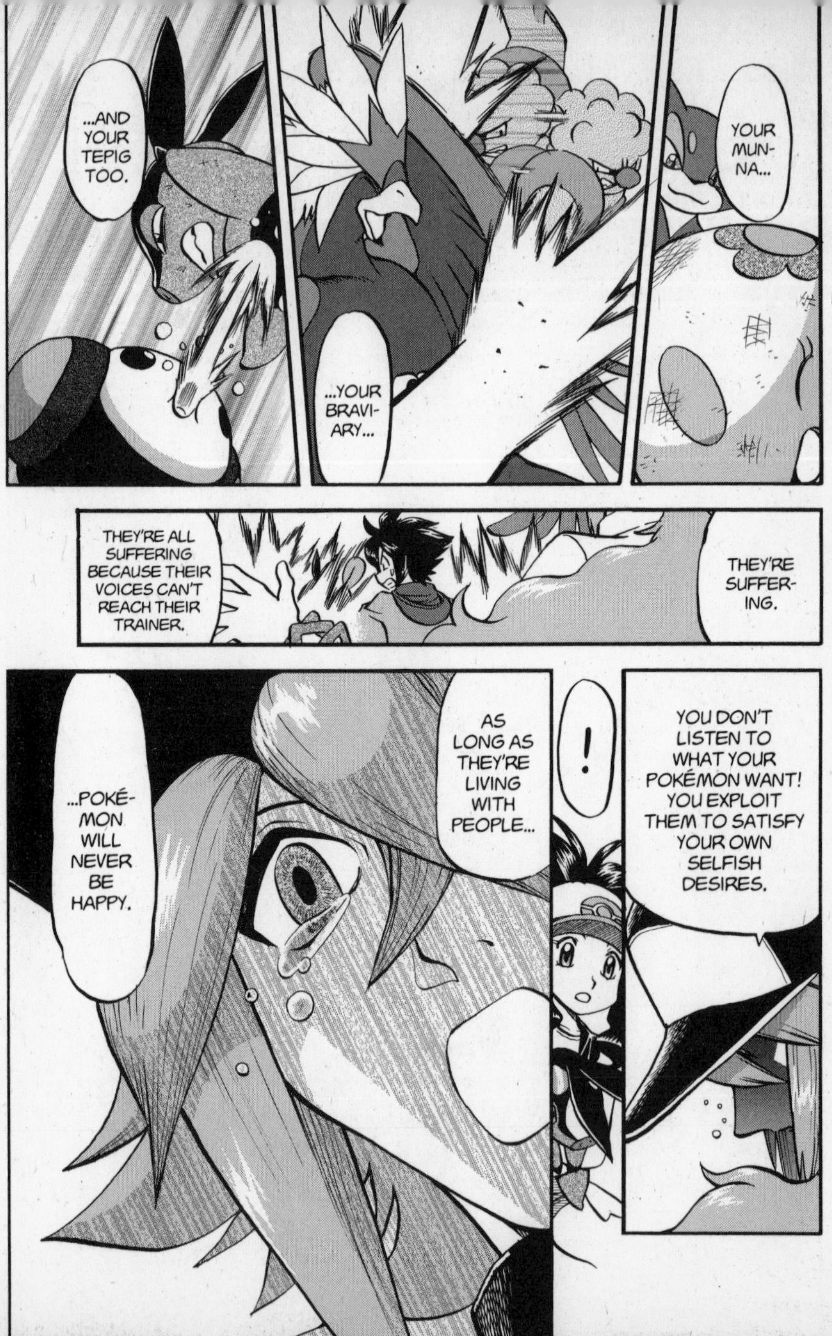
YOUR MUN-NA...
...YOUR BRAVI-ARY...
...AND YOUR TEPIG TOO.
THEY'RE SUFFER-ING.
THEY'RE ALL SUFFERING BECAUSE THEIR VOICES CAN'T REACH THEIR TRAINER.
YOU DON'T LISTEN TO WHAT YOUR POKÉMON WANT! YOU EXPLOIT THEM TO SATISFY YOUR OWN SELFISH DESIRES.
!
AS LONG AS THEY'RE LIVING WITH PEOPLE...
...POKÉ-MON WILL NEVER BE HAPPY.

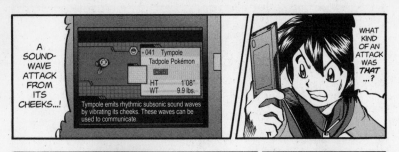

A SOUND-WAVE ATTACK FROM ITS CHEEKS...!

• 041 Tympole
Tadpole Pokémon

HT 1'08"
WT 9.9 lbs.

Tympole emits rhythmic subsonic sound waves by vibrating its cheeks. These waves can be used to communicate.

WHAT KIND OF AN ATTACK WAS *THAT*...?

THERE'S NO NEED FOR THAT. ALL YOU HAVE TO DO IS *LISTEN* TO THE VOICES OF THE POKÉMON THEMSELVES.

YOU'RE DEPENDENT ON *DATA* TO LEARN ABOUT YOUR OPPONENT'S POKÉMON.

SEE? YOU USED THAT POKÉDEX THING AGAIN.

I DON'T HAVE TO LOOK IT UP IN SOME MECHANICAL DEVICE. I HEAR THE VOICES OF POKÉMON DIRECTLY.

THAT'S HOW I KNOW WHICH MOVE TO USE AND WHEN.

AND YOUR POKÉMON AS WELL.

I'M LISTENING TO MY TYMPOLE.

...YOU CAN *NEVER* DEFEAT ME.

THAT'S WHY...

TYMPOLE.
ECHOED
VOICE.

FWEEEE
WE
E
EE
E

TEP!

WHAP

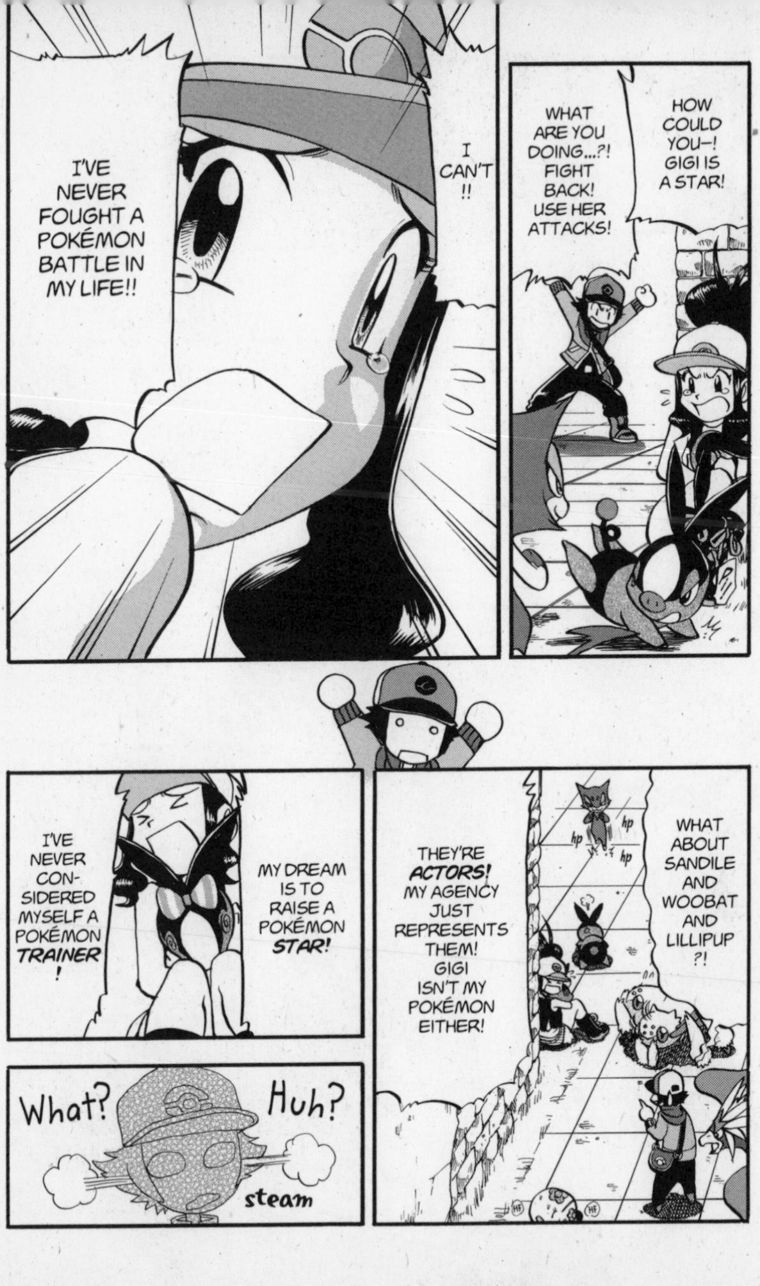

I CAN'T!!
I'VE NEVER FOUGHT A POKÉMON BATTLE IN MY LIFE!!
WHAT ARE YOU DOING...?! FIGHT BACK! USE HER ATTACKS!
HOW COULD YOU–! GIGI IS A STAR!
MY DREAM IS TO RAISE A POKÉMON STAR!
I'VE NEVER CONSIDERED MYSELF A POKÉMON TRAINER!
What?
Huh?
steam
WHAT ABOUT SANDILE AND WOOBAT AND LILLIPUP?!
THEY'RE ACTORS! MY AGENCY JUST REPRESENTS THEM! GIGI ISN'T MY POKÉMON EITHER!
hp
hp
hp

WHAA-AT ?!

IF WORSE COMES TO WORST...

...YOU'RE GONNA HAVE TO FIGHT.

AND HE KEEPS ATTACKING US?

WHAT IF THIS GUY BEATS ME... AND I'M LEFT WITH NO POKÉMON IN FIGHTING CONDITION?

YES, YOU CAN!

I CAN'T, I CAN'T, I CAN'T, I CAN'T!!

I'M JUST SAYING, YOU OUGHTA PREPARE TO DEFEND YOURSELF!

PIII!!

GIGI!

UM, BUT BLACK...

ONE MORE TIME, MUSHA!

WHAM

THOK

S/ish

Y-YES.

BOSS...

PLOP

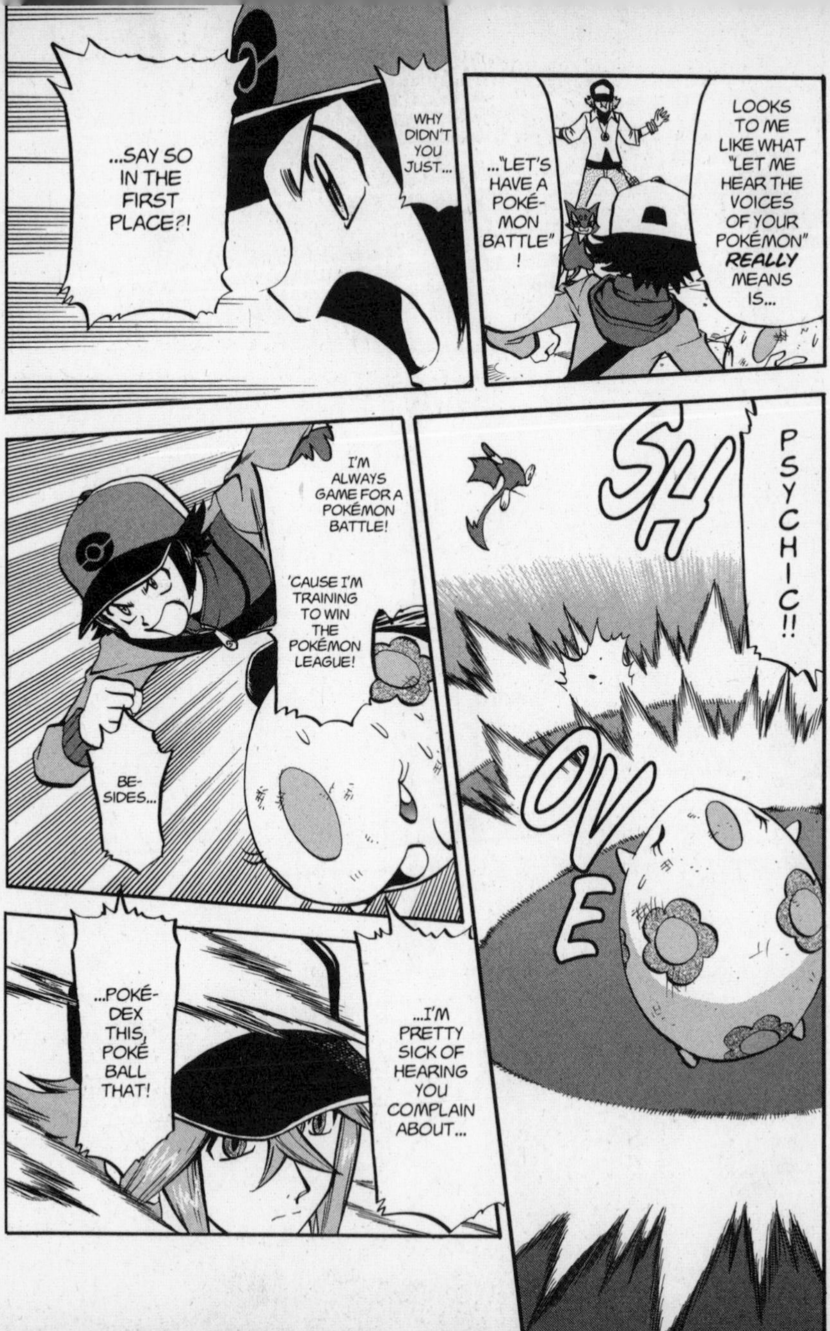
LOOKS TO ME LIKE WHAT "LET ME HEAR THE VOICES OF YOUR POKÉMON" **REALLY** MEANS IS...
..."LET'S HAVE A POKÉMON BATTLE"!
WHY DIDN'T YOU JUST...
...SAY SO IN THE FIRST PLACE?!
PSYCHIC!!
SHOVE
I'M ALWAYS GAME FOR A POKÉMON BATTLE!
'CAUSE I'M TRAINING TO WIN THE POKÉMON LEAGUE!
BESIDES...
...I'M PRETTY SICK OF HEARING YOU COMPLAIN ABOUT...
...POKÉDEX THIS, POKÉ BALL THAT!

MY NAME...

...IS N.

BEFORE THEY'RE ENCLOSED INSIDE THEIR POKÉ BALLS AND CAN NO LONGER COMMUNI-CATE...

NOW! LET ME HEAR THE VOICES OF YOUR POKÉ-MON...

THUNK

SLASH

...YOU ARE IMPRISONING THAT POKÉMON INSIDE A POKÉ BALL FOR NOTHING.

THE POKÉDEX COLLECTS DATA ABOUT POKÉMON...

IF THE ONLY REASON YOU CAPTURE A POKÉMON IS TO FILL THE POKÉDEX WITH ITS DATA...

ADMIT IT!

SO THAT'S WHAT THAT GADGET'S CALLED!

HMPH.

HOW WOULD YOU KNOW? AFTER ALL, ONCE YOU IMPRISON THEM INSIDE POKÉ BALLS, HOW CAN YOU *HEAR THEIR VOICES?*

ARE POKÉMON HAPPY INSIDE THERE?

I'M A TRAINER MYSELF, BUT I'VE ALWAYS WONDERED...

ZOOP

THAT'S RIGHT.

D'YOU REALLY THINK POKÉ BALLS AND POKÉDEXES...

...HURT POKÉ-MON?

WHO ARE YOU!?

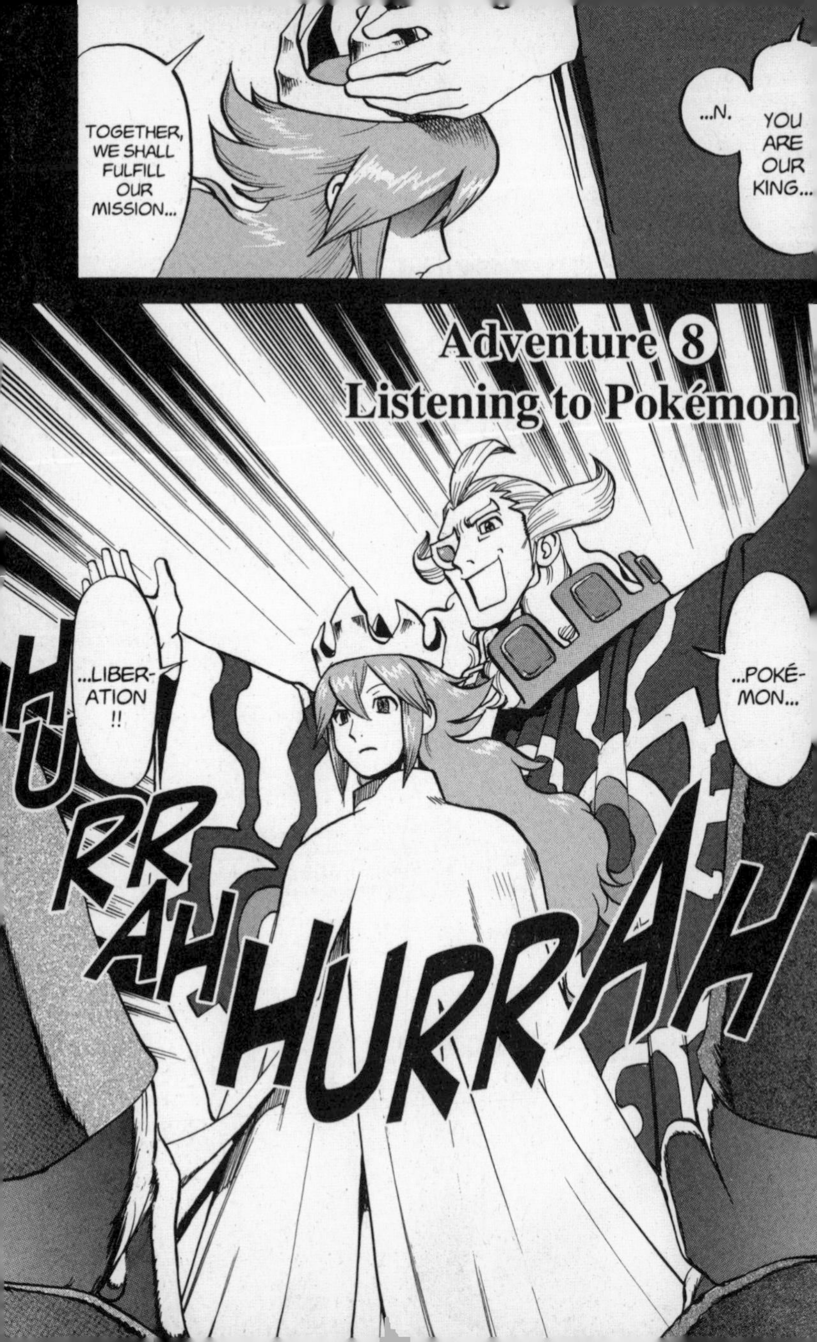
...N.
YOU ARE OUR KING...
TOGETHER, WE SHALL FULFILL OUR MISSION...
Adventure 8
Listening to Pokémon
...POKÉMON...
...LIBERATION !!
HURRAH
HURRAH

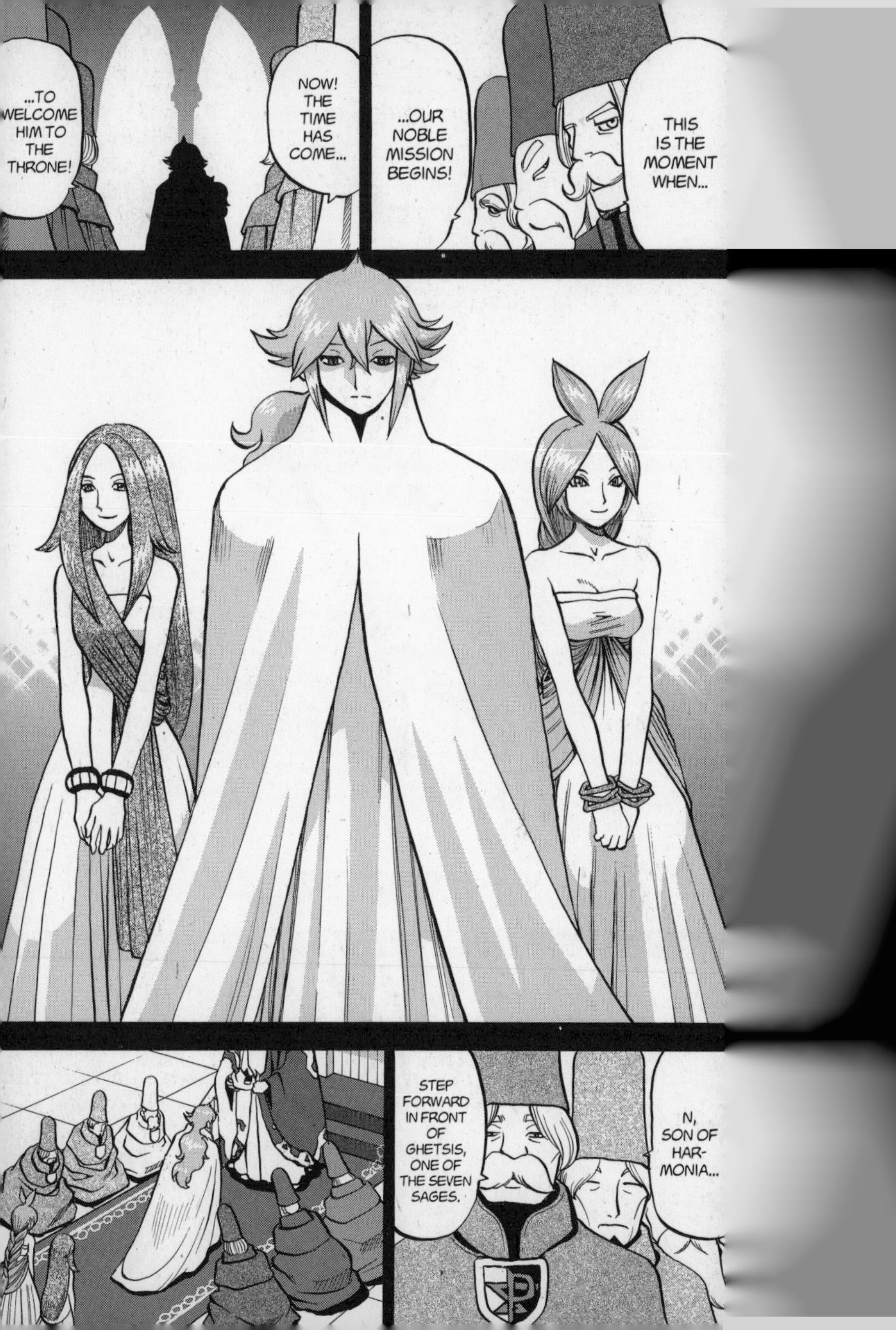
THIS IS THE MOMENT WHEN...
...OUR NOBLE MISSION BEGINS!
NOW! THE TIME HAS COME...
...TO WELCOME HIM TO THE THRONE!
N, SON OF HAR-MONIA...
STEP FORWARD IN FRONT OF GHETSIS, ONE OF THE SEVEN SAGES.

Adventure 8
Listening to Pokémon

THE CORONATION IS ABOUT TO BEGIN.

HE WHO IS ABOUT TO BE CROWNED SHALL BE LORD OF THIS CASTLE...

IN OTHER WORDS— *THE KING OF TEAM PLASMA.*

THE STORY THUS FAR!

Pokémon Trainer Black is exploring the mysterious Unova region with his brand-new Pokédex. Pokémon Trainer White runs a thriving talent agency for performing Pokémon. Traveling together, they run into Team Plasma, a group that advocates releasing your Pokémon into the wild!

Now Black is attacked by N, who has the nerve to tell Black he isn't in touch with his Pokémon's feelings. Them's fighting words—literally! Which of the two Trainers has the best relationship with his Pokémon, and will that help him win a heated Pokémon battle...?

BLACK'S dream is to win the Pokémon League!

WHITE'S dream is to make her Tepig Gigi a star!

Black's childhood friends BIANCA and CHEREN have broken Pokédexes.

Black's MUNNA helps him think clearly by temporarily "eating" his dream.

Black's Tepig, TEP, and White's Tepig, GIGI, get along like peanut butter and jelly!

N believes Pokémon should live without humans. But is that what's best...?

Pokémon

BLACK AND WHITE

VOL.3

Pokémon Black and White
Volume 3
VIZ Kids Edition

Story by HIDENORI KUSAKA
Art by SATOSHI YAMAMOTO

© 2011 Pokémon.
© 1995–2011 Nintendo/Creatures Inc./GAME FREAK inc.
TM and ® and character names are trademarks of Nintendo.
© 1997 Hidenori KUSAKA and Satoshi YAMAMOTO/Shogakukan
All rights reserved.
Original Japanese edition "POCKET MONSTER SPECIAL"
published by SHOGAKUKAN Inc.

English Adaptation / Annette Roman
Translation / Tetsuichiro Miyaki
Touch-up & Lettering / Susan Daigle-Leach
Design / Fawn Lau
Editor / Annette Roman

Printed in the U.S.A.

Published by VIZ Media, LLC
P.O. Box 77010
San Francisco, CA 94107

10 9 8 7 6 5 4 3
First printing, September 2011
Third printing, February 2013

POKéMON

™

BLACK AND WHITE

VOL.3

Story by **HIDENORI KUSAKA**
Art by **SATOSHI YAMAMOTO**